For my good friends,
Sue, Liz and Irene
~S.C.

For Aaron
~T.L.

First published in the United States 1998 by Little Tiger Press,
N16 W23390 Stoneridge Drive, Waukesha, WI 53188
Originally published in Great Britain 1998 by Magi Publications
Text © 1998 Sheridan Cain
Illustrations © 1998 Tanya Linch
All rights reserved.
Library of Congress Cataloging-in-Publication Data
Cain, Sheridan.
Look out for the big bad fish! / by Sheridan Cain
    illustrated by Tanya Linch.   p. cm.
        Summary : Tadpole is distressed because all of the animals
        he encounters can jump and he has not yet learned how,
        but the ability comes to him just at the right time.
        ISBN 1-888444-27-4 (hc)
        [1. Tadpoles—Fiction. 2. Animals—Fiction. 3. Jumping
        —Fiction.]   I. Linch, Tanya, ill. II. Title.
        PZ7. C1196Lo 1998 [E]—DC21 96-27854 CIP AC
Printed in Italy
First American Edition
1 3 5 7 9 10 8 6 4 2

Look Out
for the
Big Bad Fish!

by **Sheridan Cain**

Pictures by **Tanya Linch**

Tadpole swam in and out of the lily pads. It was warm, and he was having a wonderful time splishing and splashing.

"Hello, Tadpole," said Mother Frog
as she flopped onto a nearby lily pad.
"What a beautiful summer day!"

"What's summer, Mom?" asked
Tadpole.

"Summer is when it's warm,"
she said. "It's the best time for
frogs to leap and jump."

Boing

jumped Mother
Frog. She hopped
high into the air,
somersaulted,
and landed
with a PLOP!

"I bet *I* can do that," said Tadpole, and he tried to leap onto the lily pad where his mother sat. But all he could do was splish and splash.

"Mom, why can't I jump like you?" asked
Tadpole.
"Oh, you will, Tadpole," said Mother Frog.
"But I want to jump *now*," said Tadpole.
"When you are a little older, you will," said
his mother.

Disappointed, Tadpole swam off downstream.

"Come back soon, Tadpole!" called Mother Frog. "And look out for the Big Bad Fish!"

Tadpole wriggled his way to the edge of the
stream. Here among the buttercups it was safe.
"Hello," said a voice nearby. Tadpole looked
up and saw a woolly face with a smudgy nose.

"Hello," said Tadpole.
"Who are you?"
"I'm Lamb," said the woolly face.
"Can you jump?" asked Tadpole.
"You bet I can!" said Lamb. "Watch this!"

Boing

jumped Lamb.

"Phew!" said
Tadpole. "I wish
I could jump like that."
    "Oh, you will, Tadpole,"
said Lamb. "When you are
a little older, you will."
    "But I want to
jump *now*," cried
    Tadpole, and he swam
        sadly home.

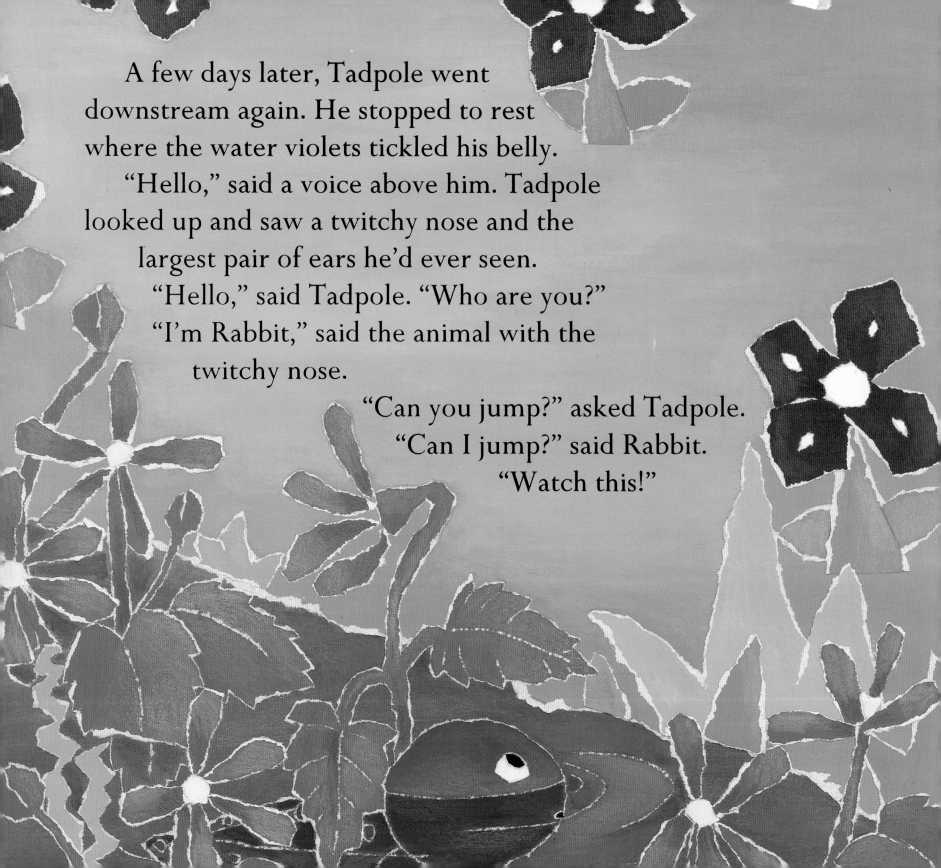

A few days later, Tadpole went downstream again. He stopped to rest where the water violets tickled his belly.

"Hello," said a voice above him. Tadpole looked up and saw a twitchy nose and the largest pair of ears he'd ever seen.

"Hello," said Tadpole. "Who are you?"

"I'm Rabbit," said the animal with the twitchy nose.

"Can you jump?" asked Tadpole.

"Can I jump?" said Rabbit.

"Watch this!"

Boing

jumped Rabbit.

"Oh my," said Tadpole. "I wish I could jump like that."

"Oh, you will, Tadpole," said Rabbit. "When you are a little older, you will."

"But I want to jump *now*," wailed Tadpole, and he swam home.

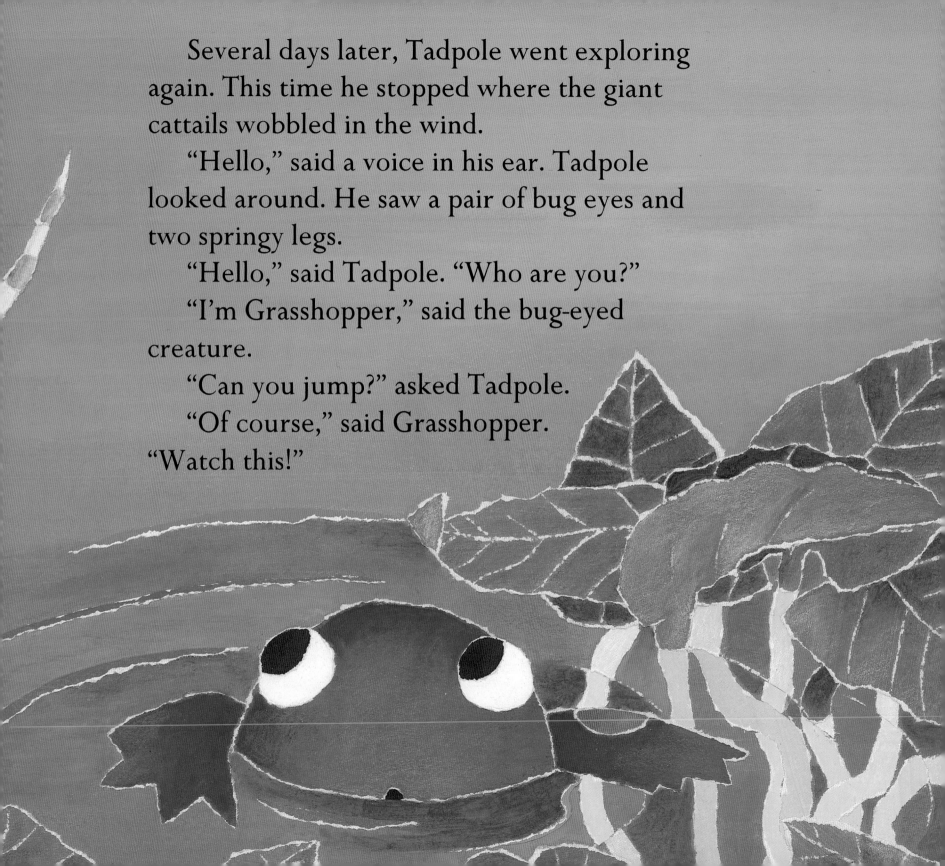

Several days later, Tadpole went exploring again. This time he stopped where the giant cattails wobbled in the wind.

"Hello," said a voice in his ear. Tadpole looked around. He saw a pair of bug eyes and two springy legs.

"Hello," said Tadpole. "Who are you?"

"I'm Grasshopper," said the bug-eyed creature.

"Can you jump?" asked Tadpole.

"Of course," said Grasshopper. "Watch this!"

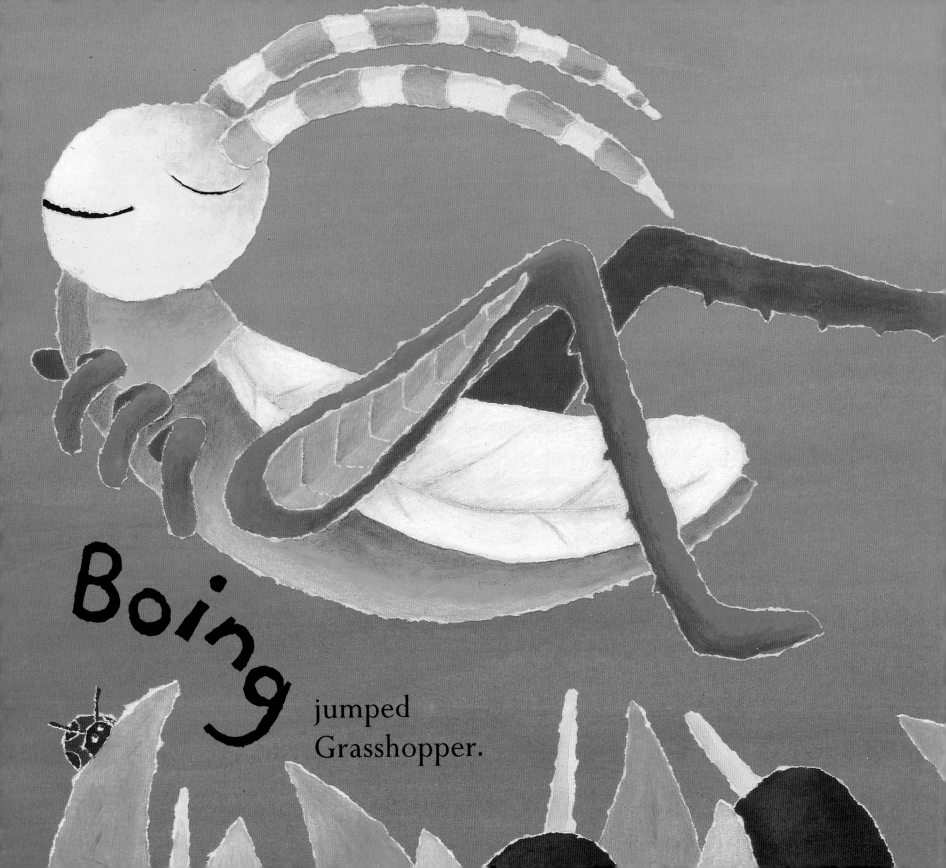

Boing jumped
Grasshopper.

"Wow!" said Tadpole. "I wish I could jump like that."

"Oh, you will, Tadpole," said Grasshopper. "When you are a little older, you will."

"But I want to jump *now*," wept Tadpole, and he swam home.

The next time Tadpole went out,
he swam farther than he ever had before.
The stream widened, and the water became deep.

"Hello," said a low voice beneath him. Tadpole
looked down and saw a pair of huge, rubbery lips.

"Hello," said Tadpole. "Who are you?"

"I'm the Big Bad Fish!" boomed the rubbery-
lipped creature.

"C-Can you j-jump?" stuttered Tadpole.

"No, BUT I *DO* EAT TADPOLES!"
said the Big Bad Fish.

Boing jumped Tadpole.

Tadpole leapt higher than Lamb.
He leapt higher than Rabbit. He even
leapt higher than Grasshopper.
He leapt all the way back home
to the lily pads.

"Look, Mom," said Tadpole,
"I *can* jump!"
Tadpole's mother smiled and
said, "What did I tell you,
Little Frog?"